The Real
Cinderella
Story

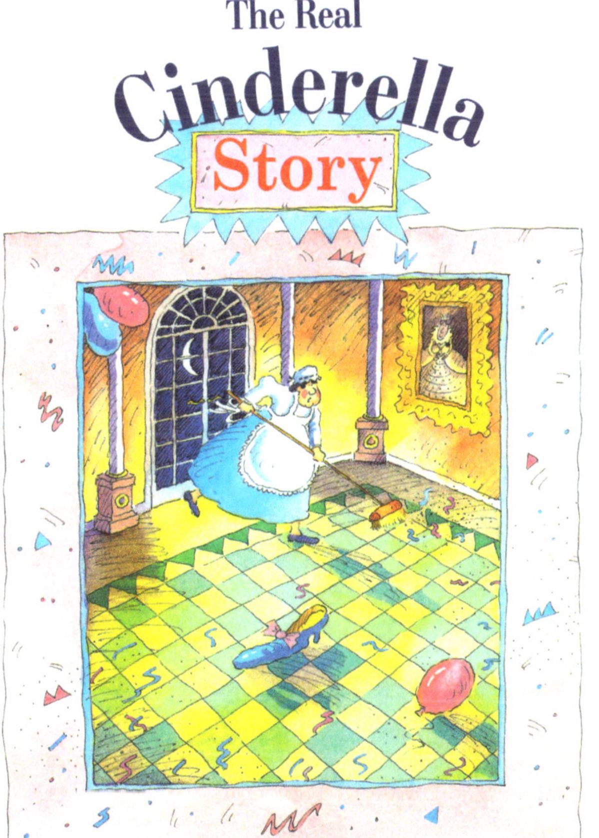

The Real Cinderella Story
The Storytellers' Club: Book 1
By Alan Trussell-Cullen

LEARNING CONNECTIONS

Learning Connections Co Ltd
Auckland, New Zealand

ISBN: 978-1-98-850589-3 Paperback format

A catalogue record for this book is available from the National Library of New Zealand.
For more information about this book, the author and the Storyteller's Club book series please contact:
Learning Connections Co. Ltd,
5 Paulange Place, Pakuranga heights, Auckland, 2010
New Zealand
Website: www.LearningConnections.co.nz
Email: AlanTC@Learningconnections.co.nz

Now, Mr Grimm was a storyteller,
And he told this story about Cinderella . . .

She's poor, and lives in a shack that's rough,
With two mean sisters that treat her tough.
Remember, I said, they were poor and all?
Yet, surprise, they're invited to the royal ball!

Now, Cinders goes to the ball as well,
But in . . . guess what? A PUMPKIN shell!
You think that's cool? You think that's nice?
The whole contraption's pulled by MICE!
And then the Prince and Cinders meet,
'Cause Cinders has the RIGHT SIZE FEET!

The whole darn yarn is just absurd.
You can't believe a single word!

3

So gather round folks, 'cause I'm goin' to tell ya
The *real* story of Cinderella!
Sorry, Mr Grimm, but I have to say,
That the story didn't start the way you say.

This'll be a shock to you, I guess,
But Cinderella was a real princess!
That's right, she was there on the royal scene,
'Cause her daddy and her mummy were the king and queen.

Now, everybody knows from storybooks,
That a princess has to have good looks—
Long gold hair and royal beauty!
They're tall and proud—and rather snooty!

But, as for Cinders, well, I guess
She just wasn't like a real princess.
She talked real loud and she giggled, too.
That's not something princesses do!

She couldn't sit still, heaven knows—
She'd be clickin' her fingers and tappin' her toes.
And as for looks, I must confess,
She didn't really look like a true princess.
She had spiked hair, and she wore bright stockings,
And the lords and ladies thought her shocking!

Now, the king and the queen, they loved their daughter,
And they did everything that parents ought to.
They hoped one day that she would marry
Some princely Tom, or Dick, or Harry.

But the royal romance just didn't occur,
'Cause the princes were all scared of her!

Now, the wisest man in all the land
Said, "King, you could try this little plan—
Gotta throw an expensive royal ball,
Invite the princes, one and all.
If the music is sweet and the lights are low,
A prince might fall for her, you know."

Well, Cinders said, "A royal gig?
That's just the kind of thing I dig!"
So they set to work to get it planned.
They bought the food and they hired a band.
They wrote to the princes, one and all,
And they all turned up at the royal ball.

The band, it sure was a hit all right.
The princes danced and jived that night.
Only trouble was, not one royal fella
Asked to dance with Cinderella!

But Cinders didn't fuss or moan.
She did a little dance all on her own.
And when the band played a song she knew,
She joined in with the singing, too.

Later in the night, the leader of the band
Said, "Hey, like to do a little drumming, ma'am?"
Cinders said, "I sure would, too!"
And she beat that drum skin black and blue!

The leader of the band said, "What do you know?
This princess drums like a real pro!
She's cool! She's hot! She's hep! She's neat!"
And everyone jived to her beat.

When the clock struck twelve, the king, he said,
"It's time they all were tucked in bed."
So the dancing music had to stop,
And they all went home from the royal hop.

After the guests had all departed,
The king and the queen sat broken-hearted.
The ball, it had drained the royal coffers,
But there hadn't been any marriage offers.

Then in the middle of the ballroom floor,
They saw this shoe, size 24.
The king said, "Wow! I've got this plan!
We'll take this shoe throughout the land.
Whoever gets his foot inside
Must have my daughter for his bride!"

But Cinders, she just laughed at this,
Which made the king quite fur-i-ous!
"Daddy, dear, don't be so twee.
That shoe you've got belongs to me!

"Besides, I really don't know why
You'd think I'd marry a royal guy?
They may be rich, they may be famous,
But everyone's an ignoramus!
I'd hate to marry a royal snob.
I think, instead, I'll get a job."

The king was stunned. "You know, my dear,
That's really not a bad idea!
You could be a chef, or a deep-sea diver,
A poet, or a farmer, or a freight-train driver!

"What about a lawyer? There's a thought!
You'd get to wear a wig in court."
Cinders gasped, "What could be dumber!
I just want to be a rock group drummer!"

The king and the queen turned sort of grey,
And they just didn't know quite what to say.
So Cinders said, "Drumming's grand!
And Neville says I can join his band."

"Well," said the king, "as a royal princess
You weren't exactly a huge success."
"That's true," said the queen, "and it is your choice.
And you do have a natural singing voice."

So she sold off her gowns and her palace frocks,
And she emptied her royal money box.
She bought this drum kit, second-hand,
And went to play with Neville's band.

Now, the band they met in this factory.
It was all run down so they got it free.
There was junk everywhere and a leak in the roof,
But at least the walls were all soundproof.

Well, they practised hard and they practised long,
And they wrote a lot of brand new songs.
They worked at their music right round the clock—
All day and night, it was rock, rock, rock.
But Cinderella didn't mind at all,
She was drumming away and having a ball.

The weeks they passed, and in good time
Their brand new songs were sounding fine.
The problem was they were getting poor,
So Neville said, "Let's do a tour!"

They bought this run-down, beat-up van,
And they tootled off across the land.
Everywhere folk danced and sang,
And Cinder's drums went bang, bang, bang!
They did these gigs all through the summer,
And the hit of the show was the princess drummer!

A record producer came along one day.
He said, "I like the way you play."
They played a song—he recorded it.
And in no time at all they had a hit.

The fans, they sang, they danced, they laughed.
They queued to get her autograph.
In fact, you could say, across the nation
The princess drummer was a hit sensation!
The king and queen were very proud
(Although they thought the music loud).

And then, one day, this programme seller
Shyly said, "Miss Cinderella,
Your drumming's great, your songs are cool.
In fact, I think you're beautiful!"

Now beautiful was not a word
That Cinderella often heard.
"Beautiful?" said Cinders, choking.
"Do you mean me? You must be joking!"

"I do mean you," the young man said.
(And, by the way, his name was Fred.)
"Beauty isn't having looks
Like people have in storybooks,
Or looking like a movie star—
It's knowing who you really are!

"You're thoughtful, warm . . . you care, you're kind.
You're frank and always speak your mind.
You're beautiful, it's really true!
I really mean it! Yes, I do!"

Cinders liked the shy, young Freddie,
And said, "Hey, man, let's go steady!"
She sang him songs. He told her jokes.
She took him home to meet her folks.

Freddie shook the hand of each,
Then Cinders gave this little speech,
"Fred's the man I really dig.
We're going to have this wedding gig."

And so our Cinders and her Fred
Became engaged and soon were wed.
And, in good time, what do you know?
They had two kids in stereo!

Now, the moral of the story that we've had so far,
You've really gotta know who you really are.
Of course you listen to what folk say,
And take advice—that's cool. Okay?
But in the end it should be you
Who must decide what you should do.

Finally, just one last word,
This may not be the tale you've heard.
But I swear as an honest storyteller,
This is the REAL TRUE Cinderella!

ABOUT THE AUTHOR

Alan Trussell-Cullen is a New
Zealand children's author, teacher,
teacher educator, and windmill
fanatic (he wants to build his own one
day!). He has written over 400 books
for children and some for teachers. (Yes, teachers read
books, too!) He also writes TV scripts and zany kids poetry.
Look out for his Good Stuff Books series, his Adventure
Kids series, his Poetry Kids series (coming soon), and other
new titles in his Storytellers' Club series.
You can find out more about Alan Trussell-Cullen and his
books on his website: **www.AlanTrussell-Cullen.com**
You can also sign up there to receive news and information
about all the new books he is working on. You'll also get news
about special offers and free stuff! (Yes, free stuff! Yea!)

WANT TO CONTACT
ALAN TRUSSELL-CULLEN?

Alan loves hearing from readers, teachers and parents.
Send him an email at: AlanTC@LearningConnections.co.nz
KIDS: say what you think about this book or ask any
questions you might have. And if you really enjoyed The
Real Cinderella Story you might even like to write a brief
review, or draw some stars to show what you think about
it. (Five stars means you really enjoyed it!) Don't forget to
give Alan your first name (or your pen name!) so he can
reply to you. You might also like to let Alan know where in
the world you live!
TEACHERS: please ask questions or share ideas and
suggestions for using this book in the classroom. Feel
free to write reviews, too. And of course, if you have your
students doing some imaginative fun things with the story
and would like to share some photos and notes, Alan would
love to see them. Above all, let's get kids reading and
writing and using their imaginations!